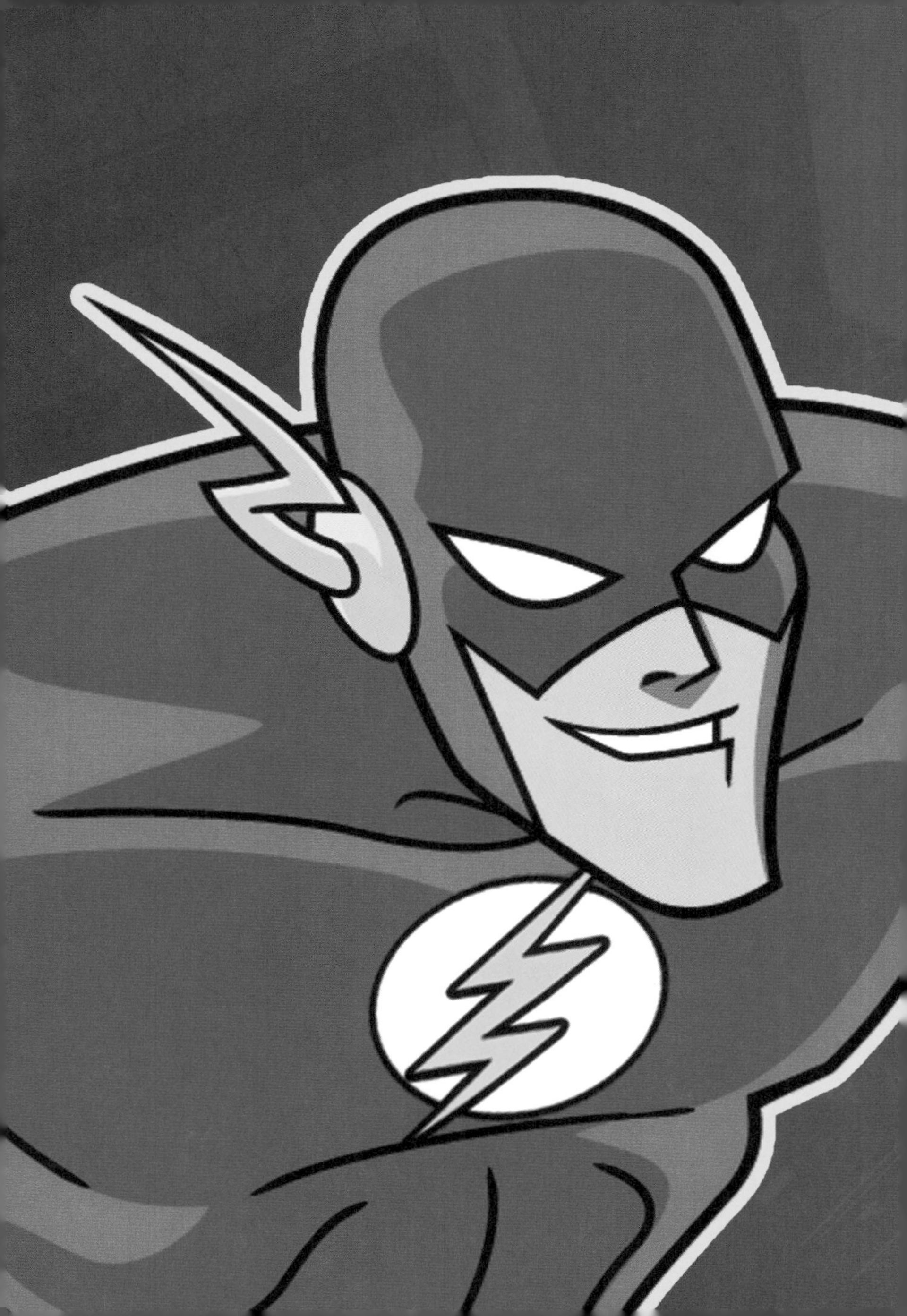

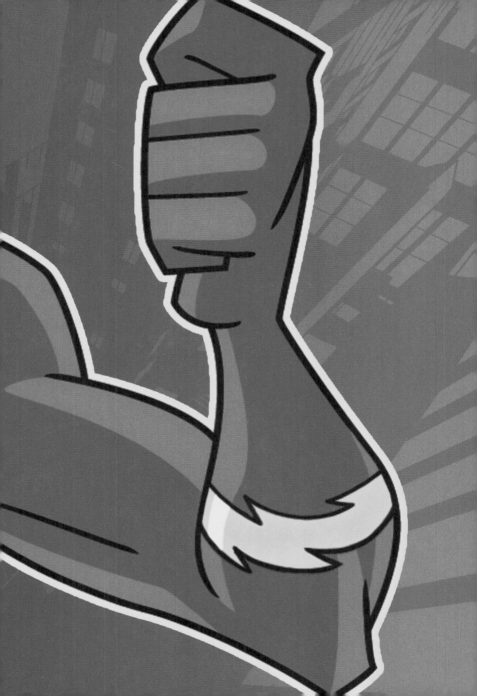

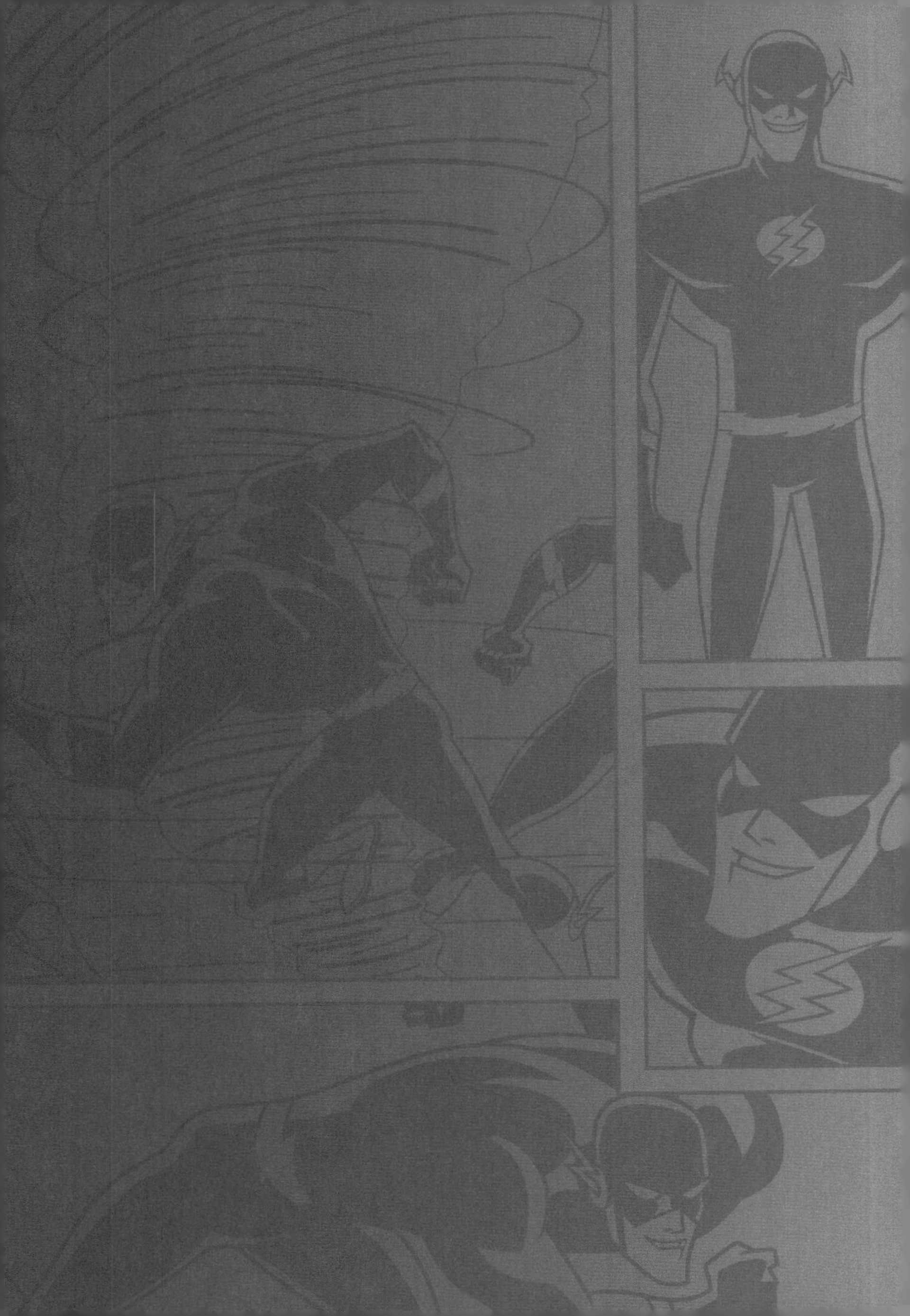

AFTER BEING STRUCK BY A BOLT OF LIGHTNING AND DOUSED WITH CHEMICALS, POLICE SCIENTIST BARRY ALLEN BECAME THE FASTEST MAN ON EARTH . . .

DC COMICS™ SUPER HEROES

The FLASH™

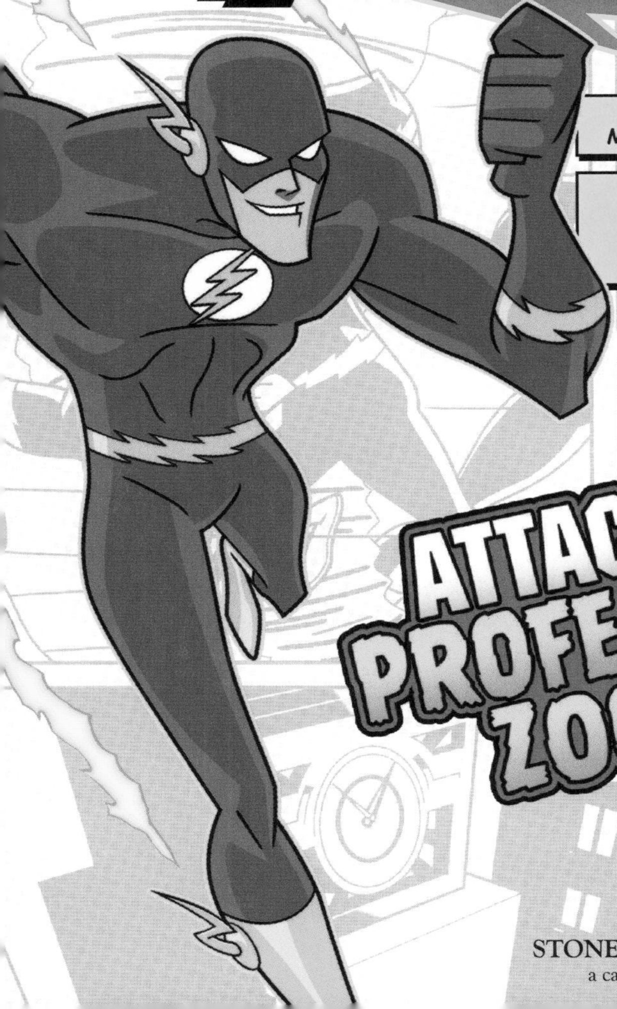

WRITTEN BY
MATTHEW K. MANNING

ILLUSTRATED BY
ERIK DOESCHER,
MIKE DeCARLO, AND
LEE LOUGHRIDGE

ATTACK OF PROFESSOR ZOOM!

STONE ARCH BOOKS
a capstone imprint

Published by Stone Arch Books
A Capstone Imprint
1710 Roe Crest Drive
North Mankato, Minnesota 56003
www.capstonepub.com

STAR13140

Cataloging-in-Publication Data is available on the Library of Congress website.

ISBN: 978-1-4342-2614-3 (library binding)
ISBN: 978-1-4342-3091-1 (paperback)

Summary: On a moonless night, downtown Central City suddenly bursts into
flames. Dozens of deadly fires threaten homes, businesses, and residents of the
metropolis. Luckily, the Fastest Man Alive is close by! The Flash rushes from
house to house, saving entire families and their pets. However, instead of being
thankful, the rescued victims accuse the Scarlet Speedster of setting the fires in
the first place. The Flash knows only one man could imitate his super-speed . .
. Professor Zoom, the Reverse-Flash! The evil super-villain is out to destroy the
real Flash's reputation and then destroy the man himself.

Art Director: Bob Lentz
Designer: Brann Garvey
Production Specialist: Michelle Biedscheid

Printed and bound in the USA.
009989R

TABLE OF CONTENTS

CHAPTER 1

IGNITION

Michael Karlin hadn't been a security guard for long. In fact, this particular evening was only his fifth night on the job. He wasn't quite used to the late hours. The warehouse district of Central City was too quiet at night. Watching over the storage facility all by himself could be a little eerie. So when Michael heard the sound of footsteps echo down the hall, he almost jumped right out of his office chair.

It's probably just the wind, he thought, grabbing a flashlight from his desk drawer.

Michael slowly crept out of his dimly lit office. There was a light coming from down the hall in the west storage hangar. Michael always double-checked the lights when he made his hourly rounds. There had to be someone in there.

Michael stepped into some sort of puddle on the floor. When he bent down to examine it, the young man caught a strong whiff of gasoline. Shining his flashlight ahead of him, he spotted a glimmering trail of the gas leading to the west hangar.

Michael swallowed nervously. This wasn't looking good. The young guard took a deep breath and tried to calm his nerves. He turned the corner at the end of the hall into the west hangar.

In front of him, a single light bulb dangled from the ceiling by its cord. The light swayed from side to side. The shadows shifted around the large room. Light flickered across tubs of experimental chemicals and tarp-covered crates.

Michael could see a man huddled in the dark far corner. The man was pouring gasoline on the floor from a large plastic container. The stranger noticed Michael and stepped into the light. Michael let out a quiet gasp despite himself. There, in the dim bulb's glow, stood the Flash.

The Flash looked over at Michael and smiled. "Better run," he said.

Before Michael could react, the Flash raced out of the room at super-speed.

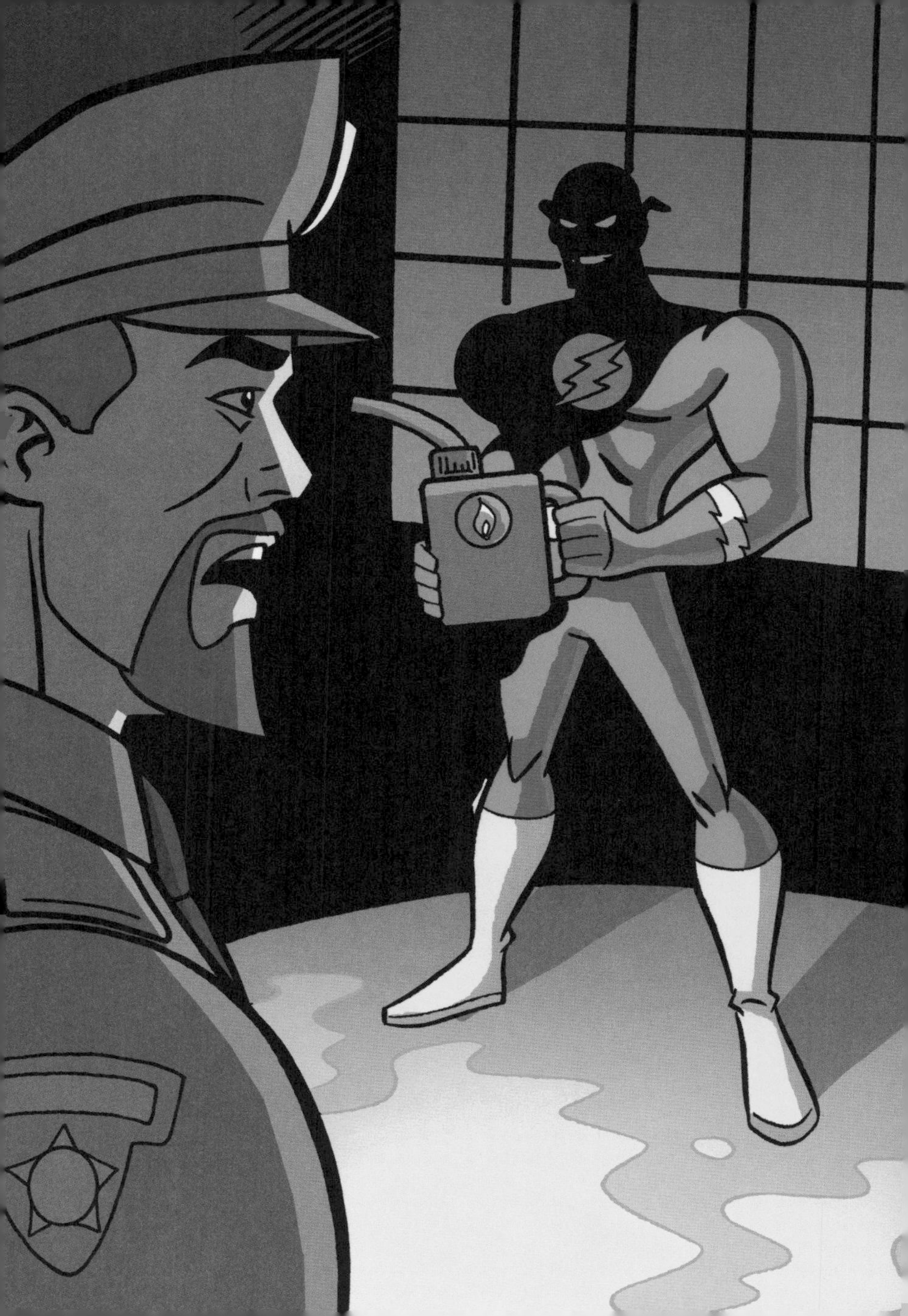

A gust of wind struck Michael and almost knocked him down. He turned to see where the Flash had gone, but had no luck. The Scarlet Speedster was quicker than Michael's eyes could follow. Michael turned back to face the empty gasoline container. He noticed that the Flash had dropped a single match on the ground nearby.

Michael's eyes went wide. Then he took the Flash's advice and ran as fast as he could.

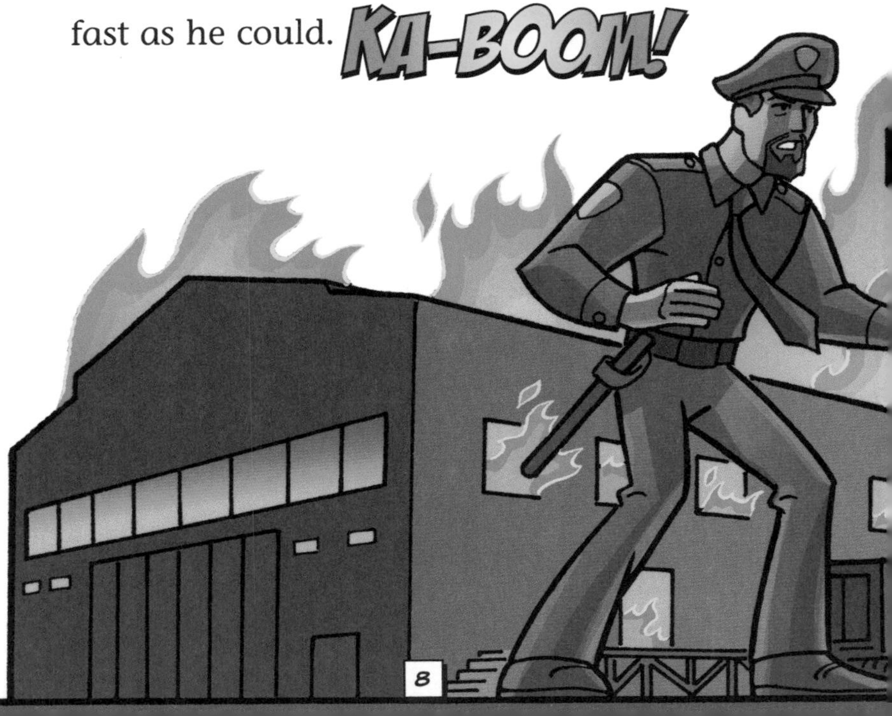
KA-BOOM!

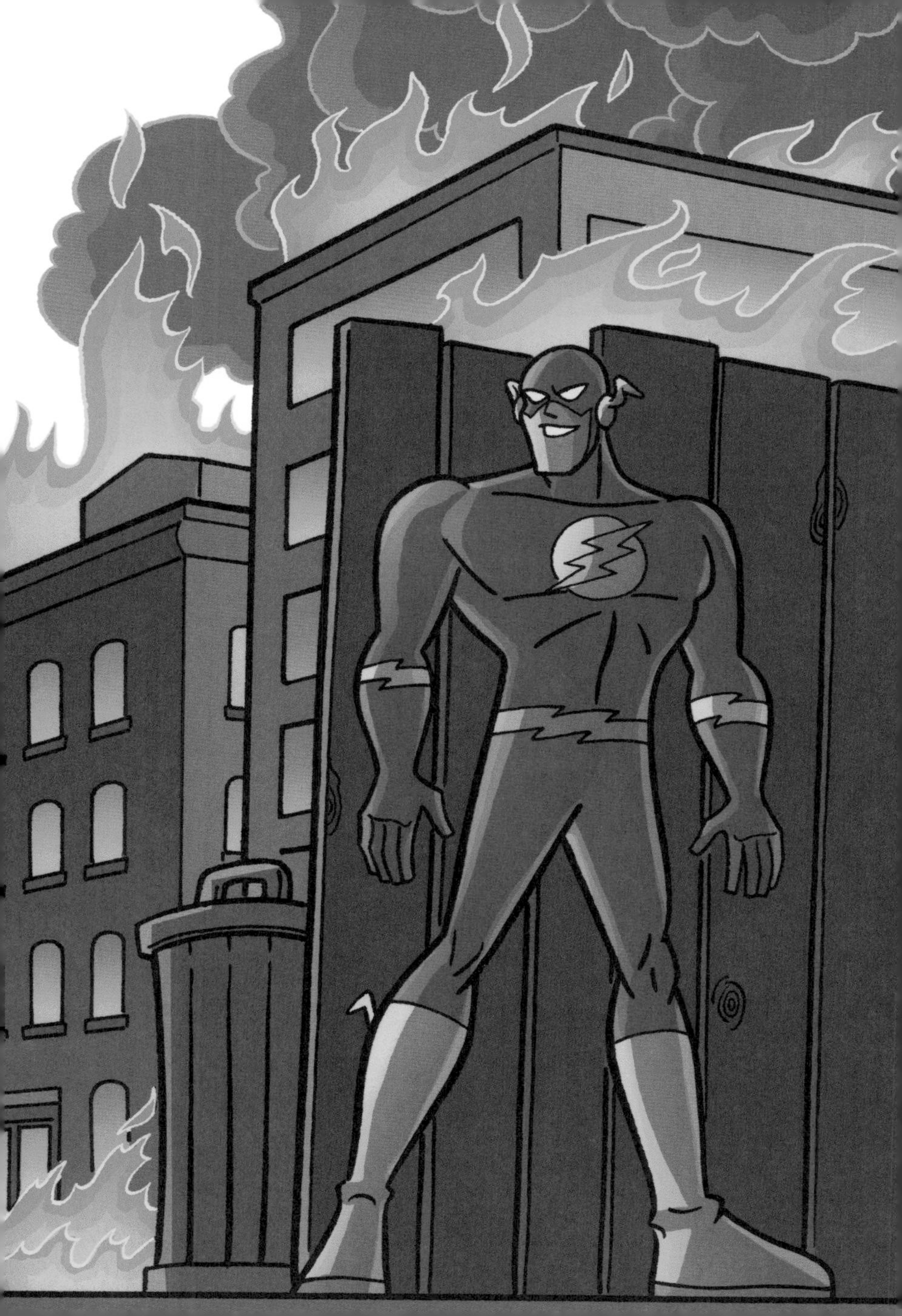

The storage hanger exploded behind Michael. The force of the blast knocked him down the hall toward the exit. The young guard quickly got to his feet.

He ran out the front door just as the hallway behind him filled with flames.

Michael stumbled onto the dark street outside. He managed to walk about a block before he realized what was happening. He froze dead in his tracks at the sight. Flames lit up the sky in all directions.

The Flash had set the entire block on fire.

CHAPTER 2

DEAD HEAT

Barry Allen was in a hurry. He raced to investigate a disturbance at the Flash Museum. This was the kind of thing that Barry took personally. After all, he'd been the Flash for years, ever since a stray bolt of lightning had struck him in his laboratory at police headquarters one stormy evening.

That night, Barry had been splashed with electricity-charged chemicals. He discovered he could move at speeds other humans only dreamed about. From that day forward, Barry Allen had served Central City as its greatest protector.

The Flash Museum was a tribute to his career. It contained dozens of weapons and death traps that his old foes had tried to use on him in the past. It housed statues and dioramas of his greatest battles. But more than that, the museum gave the city hope for a brighter future. *That* was something Barry didn't want to see destroyed.

The Flash raced down Infantino Avenue toward the Flash Museum. As he sped to the top of the avenue's famous lookout point, Barry turned to his left. The view here was always impressive, and the Flash couldn't help but catch a glimpse of it.

Suddenly, Flash stopped, spraying dirt from the street into the air. He stared out over the cityscape and saw smoke coming from the warehouse district.

Barry frowned. *The Flash Museum will have to wait,* he thought.

ZWWWOOOOMMMM! Flash rocketed at near top speed toward the smoke. Late-night pedestrians held onto their hats and jackets as they felt a sudden burst of wind. They turned to see the source of the breeze but witnessed nothing more than a quick red blur. Most shrugged and went back about the evening's business. But a few smiled knowingly. Those few understood that they'd just had a brush with greatness. Their city's hero was on the job, and Central City was in good hands.

The Flash slid to a halt in the heart of the city's warehouse district. All around him fires raged. Smoke billowed into the navy sky. On the street, a lone, wide-eyed security guard stared at the super hero.

Flash looked back at the flames. They were spreading. Barry knew that there was no time to waste — even for him.

The Flash took a deep breath. He rushed toward the first building. The door was locked. Without a moment to lose, Barry vibrated his molecules to super-speed!

ZING! Then he simply stepped through the door as if it wasn't even there.

Now safely inside, Flash stopped vibrating. He looked around the large open room. Flames blazed in every corner and on top of crates and wooden bookshelves. There was no sign of life.

Flash raced through the room, feeling the heat against his face. He sped through an open doorway into a smaller room.

Through the smoke, Flash could see a young man lying on the ground near the back wall. The man was unconscious. He had inhaled too much smoke.

Barry ran to his side in less than a second. He scooped the man in his arms and then sped toward the exit.

*   *   *

Dr. Emma Rose started her late-night rounds at the Central City Hospital. At this hour, most of her patients had been long asleep in their beds. The doctor checked their IVs and heart monitors and made sure they were comfortable. Usually, Dr. Rose had a few surprises, but this night was surprisingly quiet.

"Excuse me, doctor?" came a voice behind her.

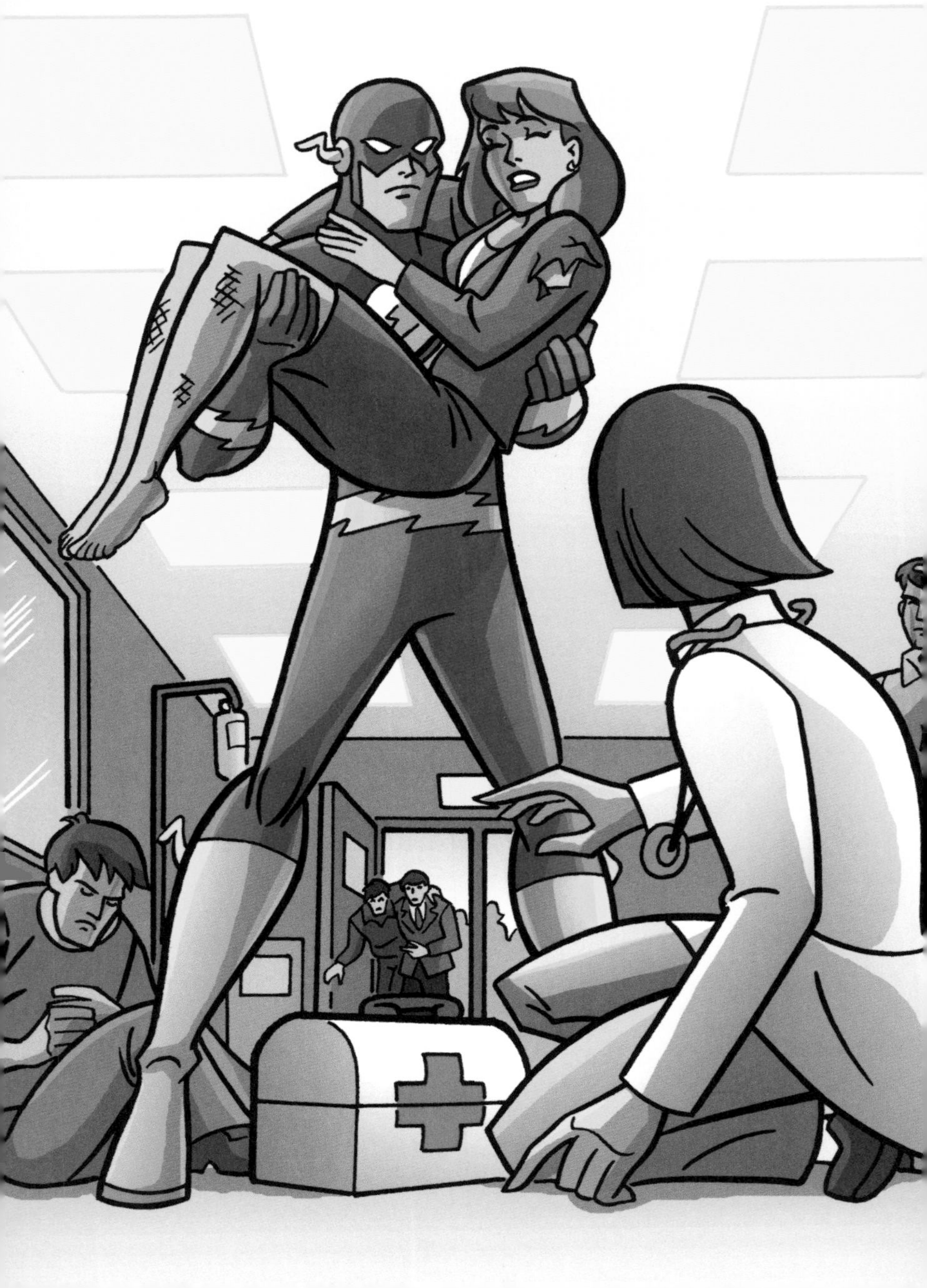

Dr. Rose turned to see the Flash holding a young woman in his arms.

"This woman needs medical attention," the Flash said.

"Oh," Dr. Rose said. "No pro —"

As quickly as he had appeared, the Flash was gone. And then suddenly, he was back again. He now held a different person in his arms.

"— blem," the doctor said, finishing her sentence.

"This lady, too," the Flash said. The young woman in the Flash's arms was coughing. "I'll be back with a lot more, so if you could get some beds or stretchers ready, that would be a big help."

The Flash dashed out of the room again.

Dr. Rose looked over at a bed that had been empty a second earlier and noticed that the Flash had laid the woman there. Across the room, on another bed, he'd placed the first young woman. The doctor rushed out of the room to alert the rest of the staff.

*   *   *

The Flash paused on the street outside the burning buildings. So far he'd carried twelve men and two women to the hospital. He had even managed to drop off a rather angry German Shepherd watchdog at a nearby veterinary clinic. He had gotten everyone to safety. Now he just needed to put out the flames.

Flash put his head down and took off around the block. Luckily, the fire hadn't spread any farther than that.

Flash continued another lap around the buildings. And then another. And then another. As Flash increased his speed, people began to gather on the streets nearby. The Flash whipped by them again and again and again.

Slowly, a funnel of air began to form around the empty burning buildings. The funnel began to grow steadily in size. As the Flash raced around the block, the whirlwind took shape. It looked almost like an enormous tornado. Smoke poured out of the funnel's spout and up above the buildings into the sky. As the funnel got larger, so did the amount of smoke.

Suddenly the Flash stopped, and the funnel began to evaporate.

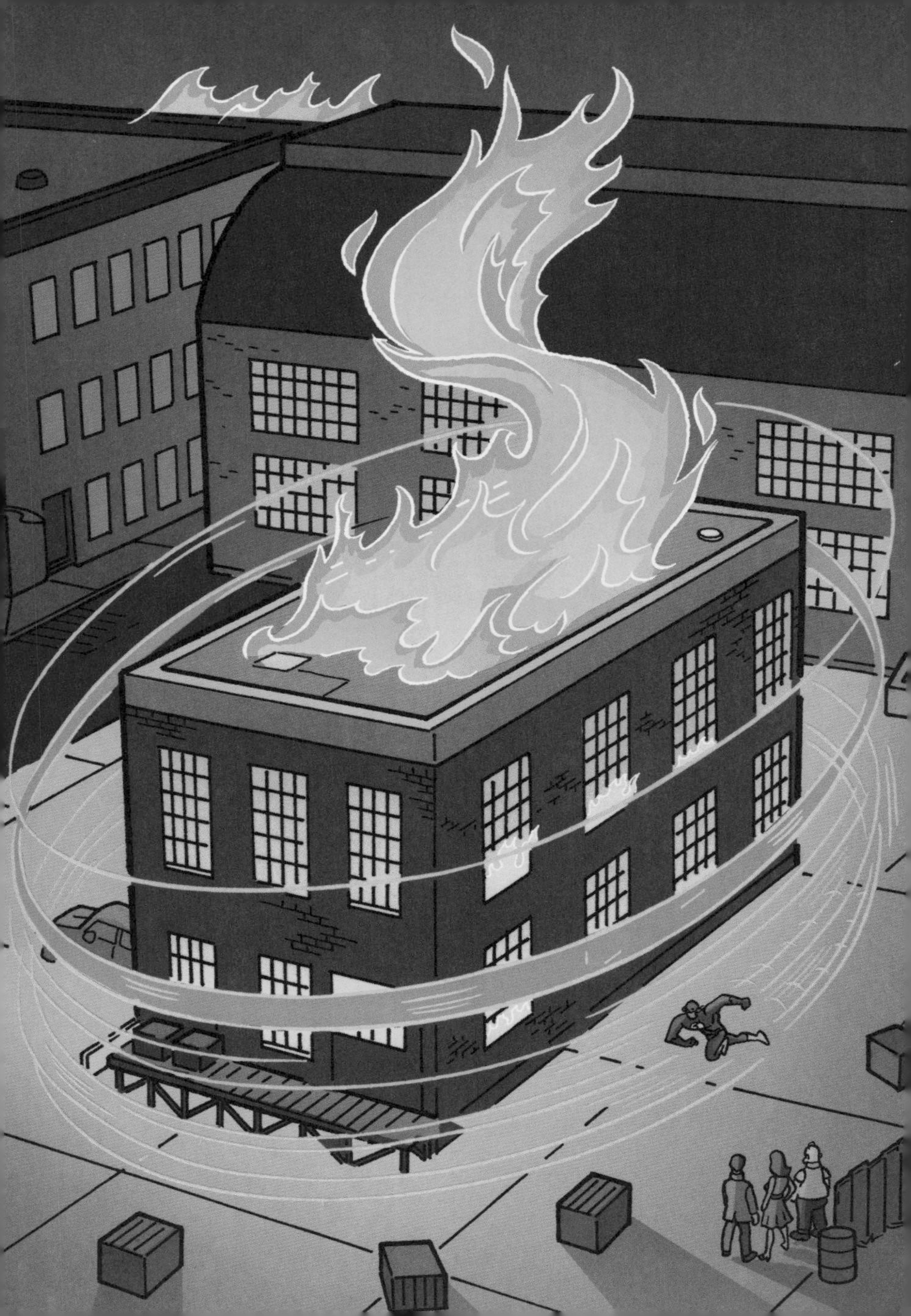

By running in a large circle, the Flash had managed to suck all the oxygen right out of the buildings. Without air to fan the flames, the fire had gone out. All that remained was a trickling trail of smoke.

Barry Allen raced over to the crowd of onlookers. He gave them a quick wave and a smile. But as he turned to speed away, he heard a voice call to him from behind.

"Where do you think you're going?" a man said.

Flash turned to face an angry security guard. The man's ID badge read "Michael Karlin."

"I saw you set those fires," Michael said.

"What?" the Flash exclaimed. *Obviously this man is confused,* he thought.

"You're not a hero," Michael said.

"So you saved everybody," the angry man added. "So what? You wouldn't have had to save anybody at all if you hadn't started this whole thing in the first place."

"I'm not sure what you mean —" Flash started to say.

"Don't play innocent," another man said from the crowd. He took a step forward. "I saw you too. You were pouring gas on the outside of the those buildings."

"I don't know what you're talking about," said the Flash.

"I'm calling the police," said a woman standing next to Michael. She pulled her cell phone out of her purse.

The Flash was speechless. He had absolutely no idea what was going on.

CHAPTER 3

TAILGATING

BEEP! BEEP! BEEP!

Flash turned to look behind him. An alarm sounded a few blocks away. The speedy super hero looked back at the angry crowd. He didn't have time for this right now. Innocent people could be in danger. So the Flash turned and ran away.

The Flash couldn't run fast enough. Central City had erupted into chaos. There had been a robbery at the Second National Bank. The perpetrator had simply vibrated *through* the vault door!

Pedestrians everywhere were getting their belongings stolen by a moving red blur. Fires were being lit all across town at record speeds. If Barry Allen didn't know better, he'd swear that only the Flash could cause this particular brand of havoc.

But he *did* know better. Someone was impersonating him. Some impostor was wearing a Flash costume and causing this string of crimes. But try as he might, the Flash just couldn't seem to catch up to him.

Flash raced from crime scene to crime scene, but he was always a moment too late. As he sped across the raised Broome Parkway, the Flash finally caught his first break. The parkway was fairly empty at night so Flash could see it clearly. An armored van was heading down the highway away from the center of the city.

The Flash caught up to the van and kept pace with it. There were two armed guards in the vehicle's front seat. It confirmed Barry's suspicions. The van was obviously carrying a lot of money.

This would be a perfect target for the impostor Flash, the real Flash thought.

Suddenly, the Flash felt a shove from behind. The force caught him off balance. Barry tripped over his own feet and began to tumble across the parkway's concrete at a tremendous speed.

He finally came to a stop. The Flash stood up and dusted himself off. He'd surely have a few bruises in the morning.

BEEP! BEEP! A car was heading right for the Flash. He was still standing on the parkway, after all.

Flash stepped to the side quickly, and the car narrowly missed him. He turned around. Someone had shoved him. At the speeds he was moving, it had to be the Flash impostor. But this time, the super hero wasn't going to let him get away.

The Flash started to run. He sped ahead of the traffic until he had almost caught up with the armored van. The Flash impostor was nowhere in sight, but it must have been him. He was sure of it.

CLANK! The steel back doors of the armored van sprang open. Flash smiled. He shouldn't have doubted himself. In the back of the vehicle stood the impostor Flash. His costume was identical to real Flash's. It was a *perfect* replica.

No wonder the public was fooled so easily, the Flash thought.

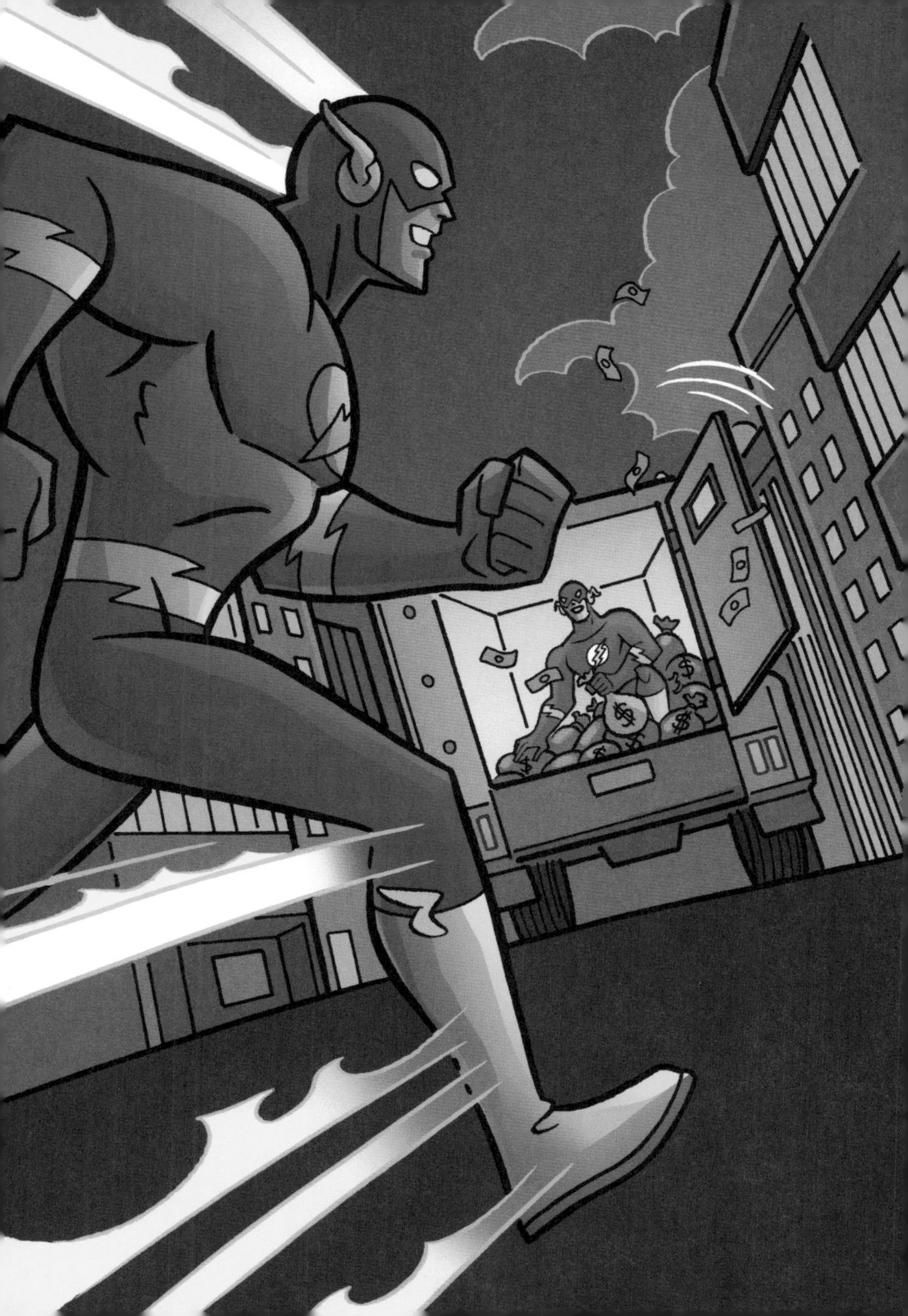

The impostor Flash was holding several cloth bags full of money. What was worse, the villain was smiling. He seemed confident that he would make his escape. The Flash wasn't quite so sure.

The hero ran behind the truck. He was waiting for the fake Flash to make a move.

"Took you long enough," the impostor said from the back of the van.

The Flash recognized the voice. It wasn't a surprise. Only one man could commit these kinds of crimes — the super-speedster from the future, Professor Zoom, also known as the Reverse-Flash.

"Zoom!" Flash said. "I knew it."

"Quite the detective, aren't you?" Professor Zoom said. His smile widened. "How do you like the new costume?"

"This is over," the Flash said. He wasn't amused by Zoom's little show.

"Not quite," Zoom said. "I've already pretty much destroyed your precious reputation. You should see the news channels. You're the most wanted man in Central City. But I've still got something extra special planned for you."

The Flash was tired of games. The Reverse-Flash was obsessed with revenge. There was nothing to be gained by talking with him. He increased his speed and jumped onboard the van. But Zoom reacted just as quickly. The villain raced out the back of the armored vehicle. He sped across the parkway's pavement. And then he abruptly stopped in front of the van. Inside the vehicle, the driver's eyes went wide. He panicked and spun the wheel to the side.

CRUNCH! The van collided with the concrete ledge of the parkway.

The Flash followed Zoom, but he was too late. The van had come to a stop. It was teetering over the overpass's ledge. Any second, it looked like it could tip over more and plunge five stories to the busy intersection below.

Flash could see the guards in the van's front seat. They looked terrified.

At the speed of thought, the Flash raced over to the parkway's ledge. He quickly threw open the van's side door. The guards didn't even have time to react. The next thing they knew, they were standing safely on the side of the parkway.

"You guys okay?" the Flash asked.

Flash looked at the armored van. It was tipping over the ledge.

"Excuse me," Flash said as he raced toward the highway off-ramp. The Flash sped to the intersection below. Cars were stopped at a traffic light, waiting patiently for their turn to drive.

Flash stopped directly under the light. He looked up. A dark shadow fell over him. The van was falling directly toward him.

"Everybody move!" the Flash yelled at the stopped traffic.

He pointed his arms at the falling truck. Flash began making little circles with his hands in the air. His arms moved so fast that they were barely visible. Wind rushed from his hands at near hurricane-like speeds.

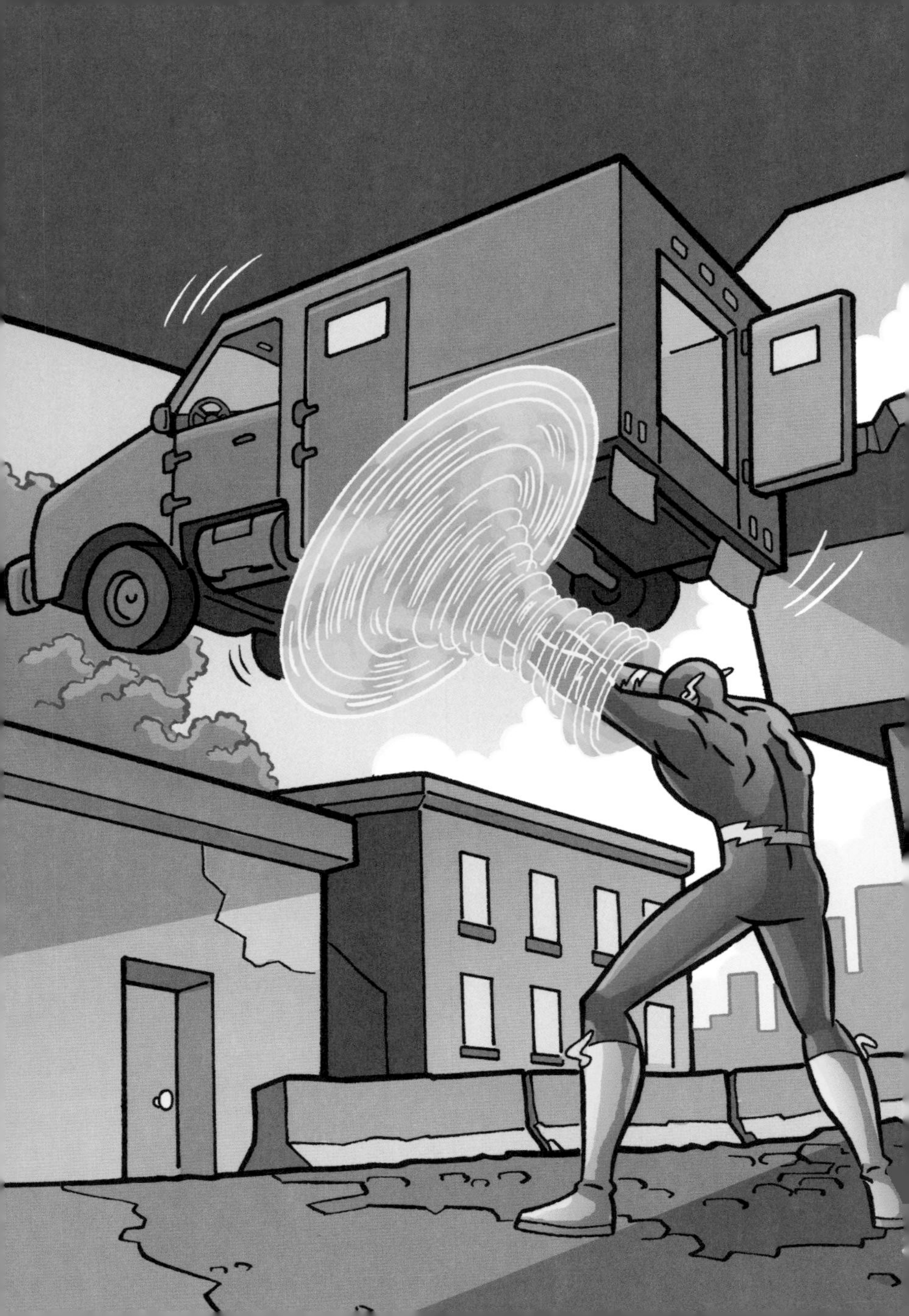

Almost magically, the van began to hover in the air directly above the Flash's head. "I said move!" Flash yelled again. The drivers that were stopped at the intersection got out of their cars. They ran away in a panic.

The Flash strained. He put all the energy he had into keeping the armored van afloat. The wind he had created wouldn't hold it for long. Finally, the feat was too much for him. Flash darted out of the way just as the van came crashing down.

Flash let out a sigh of relief. He had managed to stall the vehicle's fall just enough to make sure that the guards would not be injured.

Barry collected his thoughts.

All night Flash had been running around the city with no plan. Barry needed to think everything through. He needed to think like a policeman. Professor Zoom's Flash costume wasn't something he could pick up at a costume store. It was too perfect. And there was only one place that had a costume like that on display.

"The Flash Museum!" the Scarlet Speedster exclaimed.

It was time to retrace Zoom's steps and look for clues. And there was no better place to start than at the beginning.

CHAPTER 4

SPEED TRAP

SKREEEEEEEECH!

The Flash's yellow boots skidded to a stop outside the Flash Museum. The alarm was sounding.

Was this still the same disturbance from earlier, or had the Reverse-Flash returned to the scene of his crime? Flash wondered.

Barry raced up to the building's front doors. He typed a combination on the building's keypad. The Flash Museum had entrusted him with their security codes years ago. After all, he was always donating new exhibits to them.

The alarm shut off. Everything was quiet again. Flash raced inside the museum's doors. Despite how still everything seemed inside the building, he knew things were about to get very loud.

Barry's first stop was the security control room on the first floor. The room had cameras covering every inch of the museum. If the Reverse-Flash was in the building, the Flash could find him easily.

Sure enough, the Flash spotted his impostor on the second floor of the east wing. Zoom was in the Mirror Master exhibit. He was standing in a small, mirrored chamber. It wasn't much larger than a dressing room at a department store. Flash recognized it immediately. It was a death chamber the Mirror Master had once trapped him in.

Two of its walls had been built to operate on a track and move together in order to crush their victim. At the time, the Flash had simply vibrated through them and caught the Mirror Master unaware. But now the Reverse-Flash was standing in the chamber. It was like he was bait for a trap.

The Flash typed a few commands into the keyboard. It was time to stop playing Zoom's game and start doing things his way. In the blink of an eye, Flash disappeared from the monitor room. In a blur, he reappeared on the very screen he had been examining. It was time to confront the Reverse-Flash face to face.

*   *   *

Professor Zoom stood in the small room and smiled. Everything was going according to his plan.

Zoom blinked, and suddenly the Flash was standing directly in front of him. "I was waiting for you," Zoom said.

"I kind of figured as much," the Flash answered.

"Let's get this over with, why don't we?" the Reverse-Flash said. The Flash didn't need another invitation. His fist sailed through the air at lightning speed.

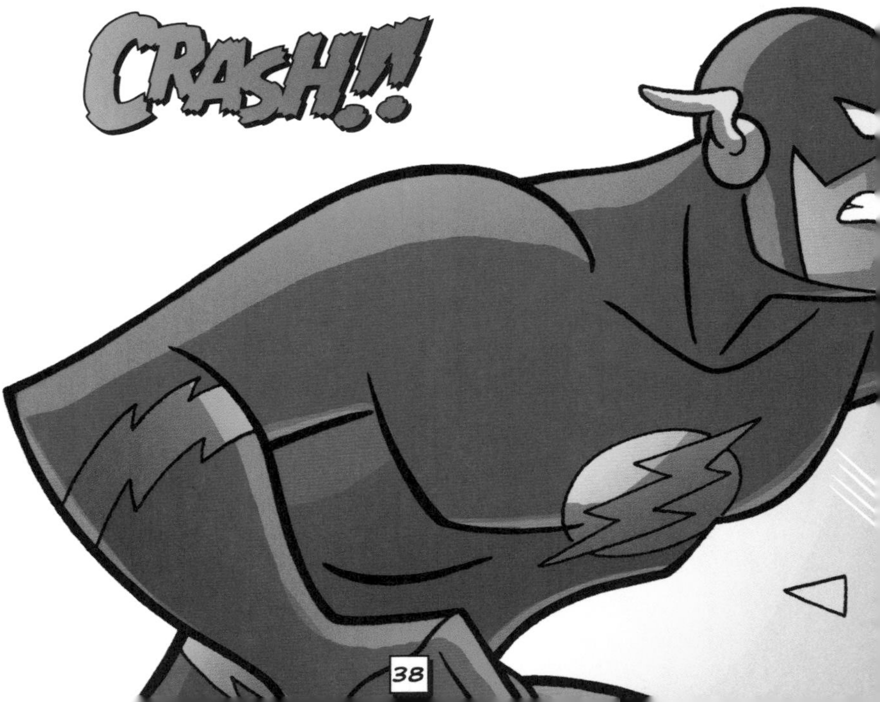
CRASH!!

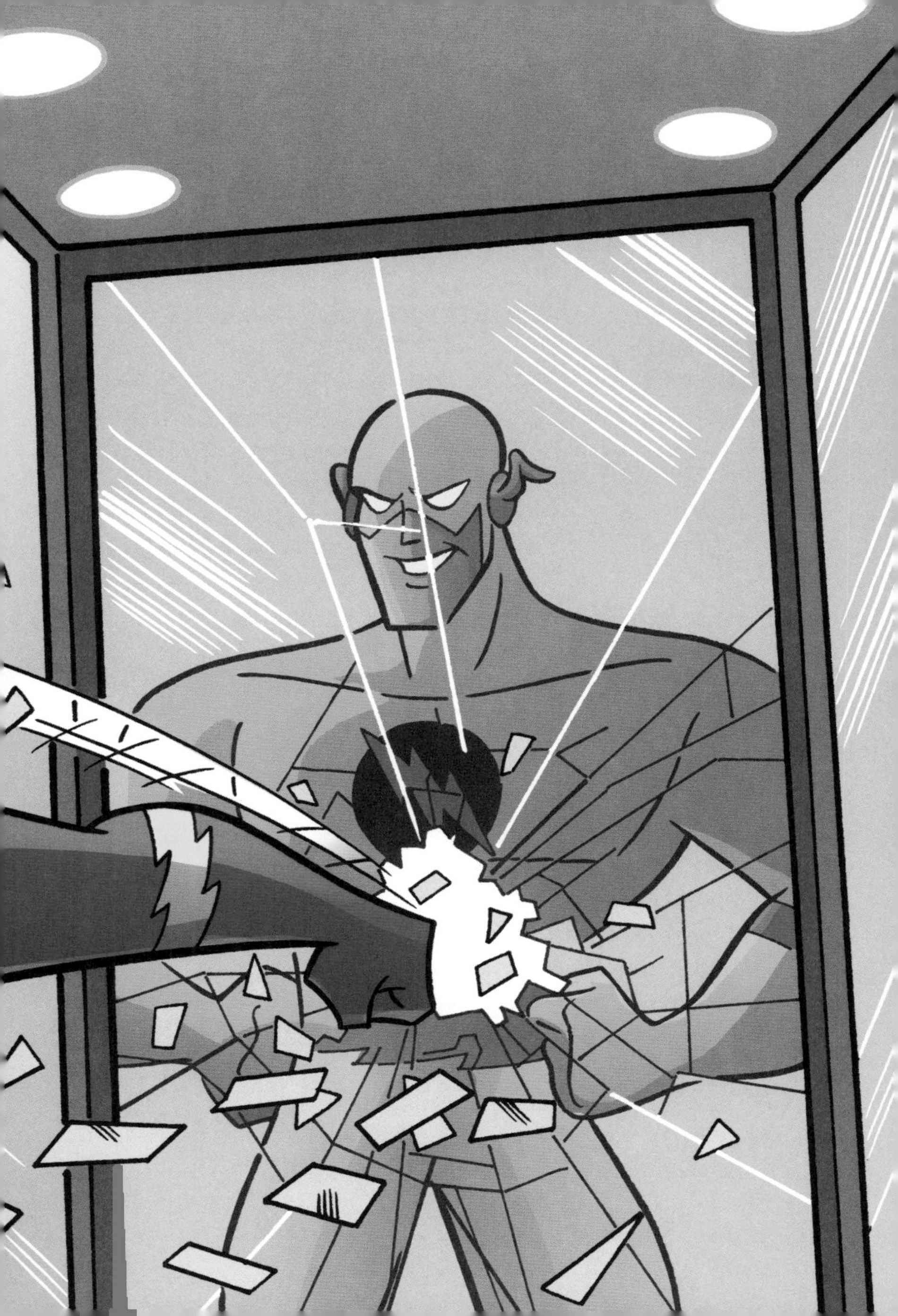

The Reverse-Flash shattered and fell to the ground in hundreds of pieces. It hadn't been Zoom at all. It was just one of the Mirror Master's trick mirrors. Flash heard a **CLICK!** He turned around to see the chamber door shut behind him. Barry was now locked inside!

"This didn't work the first time, Zoom," Flash yelled.

"Oh, I've made a few improvements," Zoom's voice echoed through the chamber. "It's one of the many perks of coming from a future time."

The Mirror Master's trap sprang to life. Two of the mirrored steel walls on opposite sides of the Flash slowly began to move forward.

Barry started to vibrate at super-speed. He moved closer to one of the walls and attempted to pass through it.

Nothing happened. The walls were still closing in on him.

"You see," Zoom said, "this machine is vibrating as well. I've made a few modifications to the original design."

"The chamber's own vibrations are constantly changing speeds to adjust to yours," Zoom explained. "The more you vibrate, the more power it pulls from the building's electrical system. I'm afraid the technology I've added will make it quite impossible for you to escape."

Flash's eyes narrowed. He hadn't planned for this. The walls were getting closer. They were almost touching him.

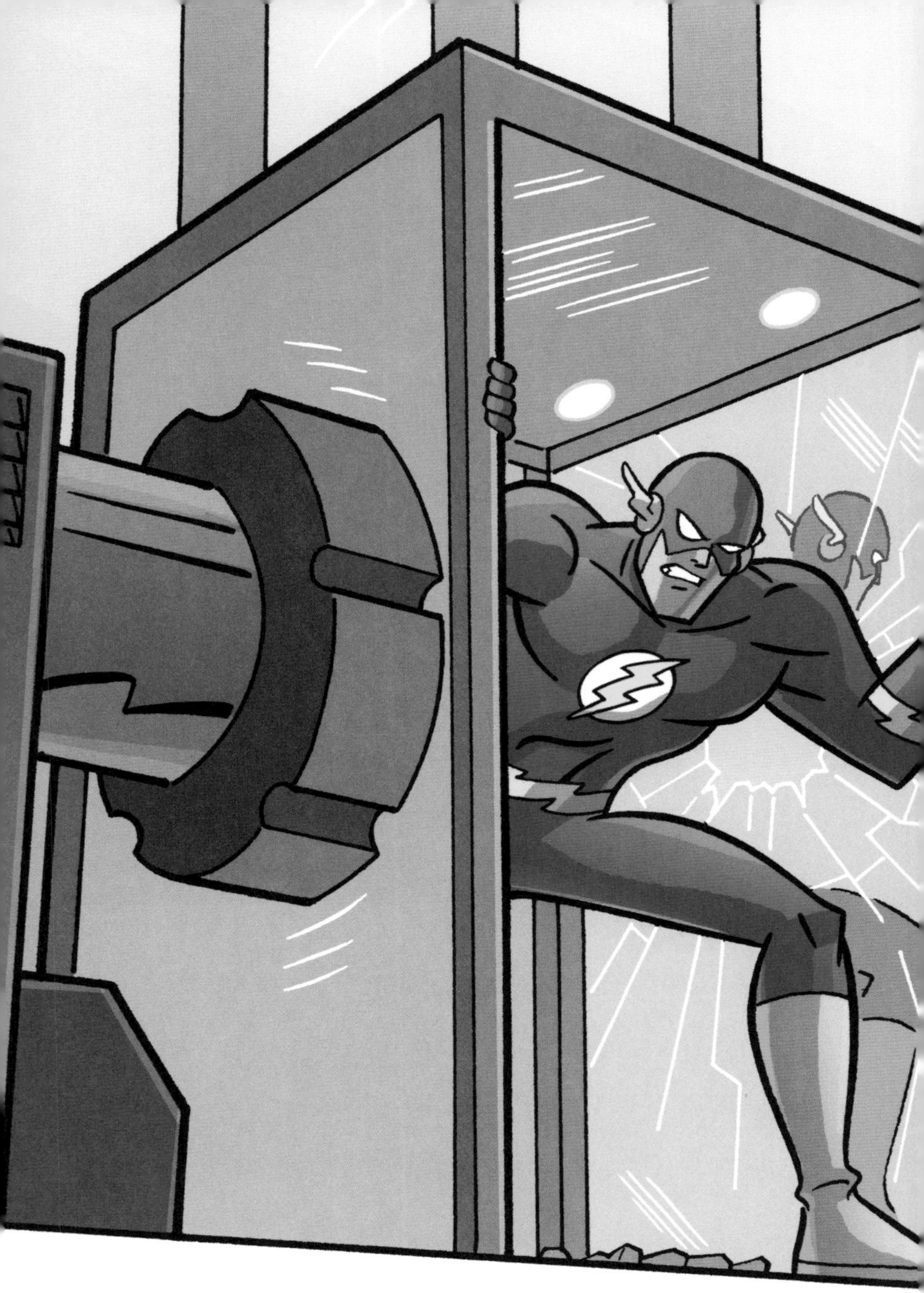

"I've destroyed your reputation, Flash," Zoom said. "And now, well, you're all I have left to get rid of."

The mirrored steel walls pressed against the Flash's chest and back. They continued to close in. He took a pained breath. He could feel the life being crushed out of him.

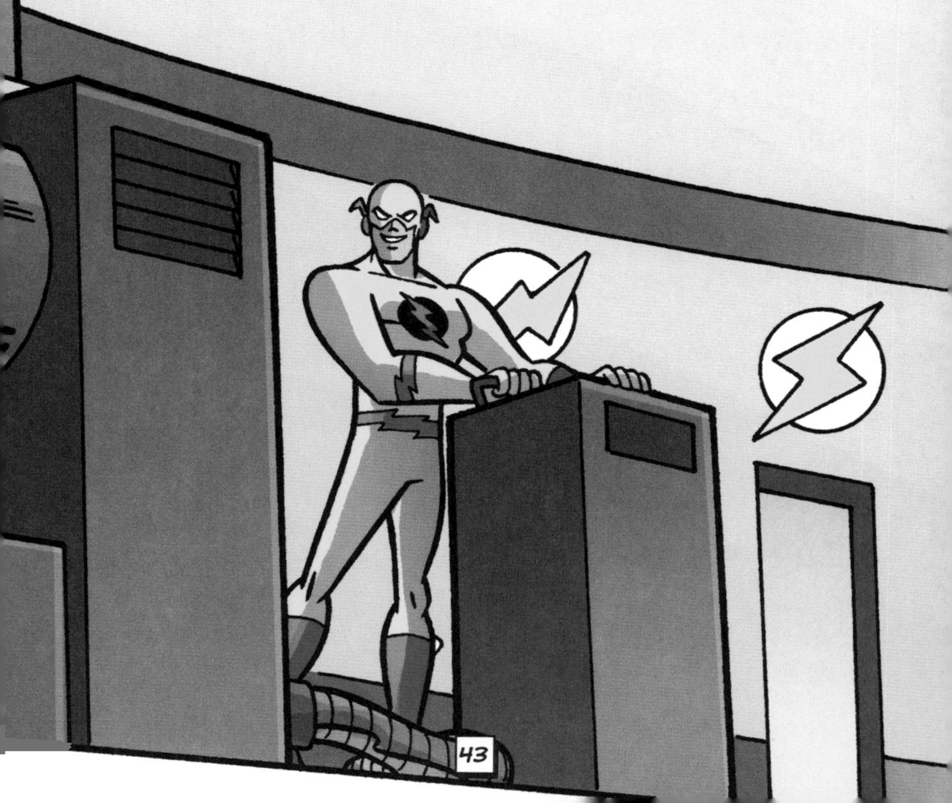

CHAPTER 5

PHOTO FINISH

ZWWMOOOOMMMM!

Flash started to vibrate faster than before. His body became a red blur. The walls continued to inch forward.

"It won't work," Professor Zoom said from outside the chamber. "The machine will just use more power. Just give up!"

The Flash wasn't listening. He could feel the walls closing in. He vibrated even faster.

It felt like Barry's body was going to simply shake itself apart. Outside the chamber, the Reverse-Flash was grinning.

"This is much more fun than —!" he started to say as the room's lights flickered. "Wait, what?" Zoom said to himself. Suddenly, the lights went out completely.

And just as quickly, they switched back on just in time for the Reverse-Flash to see a red fist speeding toward his face. **WHAM!** The force of the impact knocked him across the room. His body shattered a large mirror behind him. He looked up to see the Flash standing over him.

"Your machine couldn't keep up with me. Or rather, the building couldn't supply it with enough power. It couldn't handle that kind of surge," Flash said. "But do you know what it *can* handle, Zoom?"

Professor Zoom didn't answer. He was still struggling to stand up. Barry's punch had been too much for him.

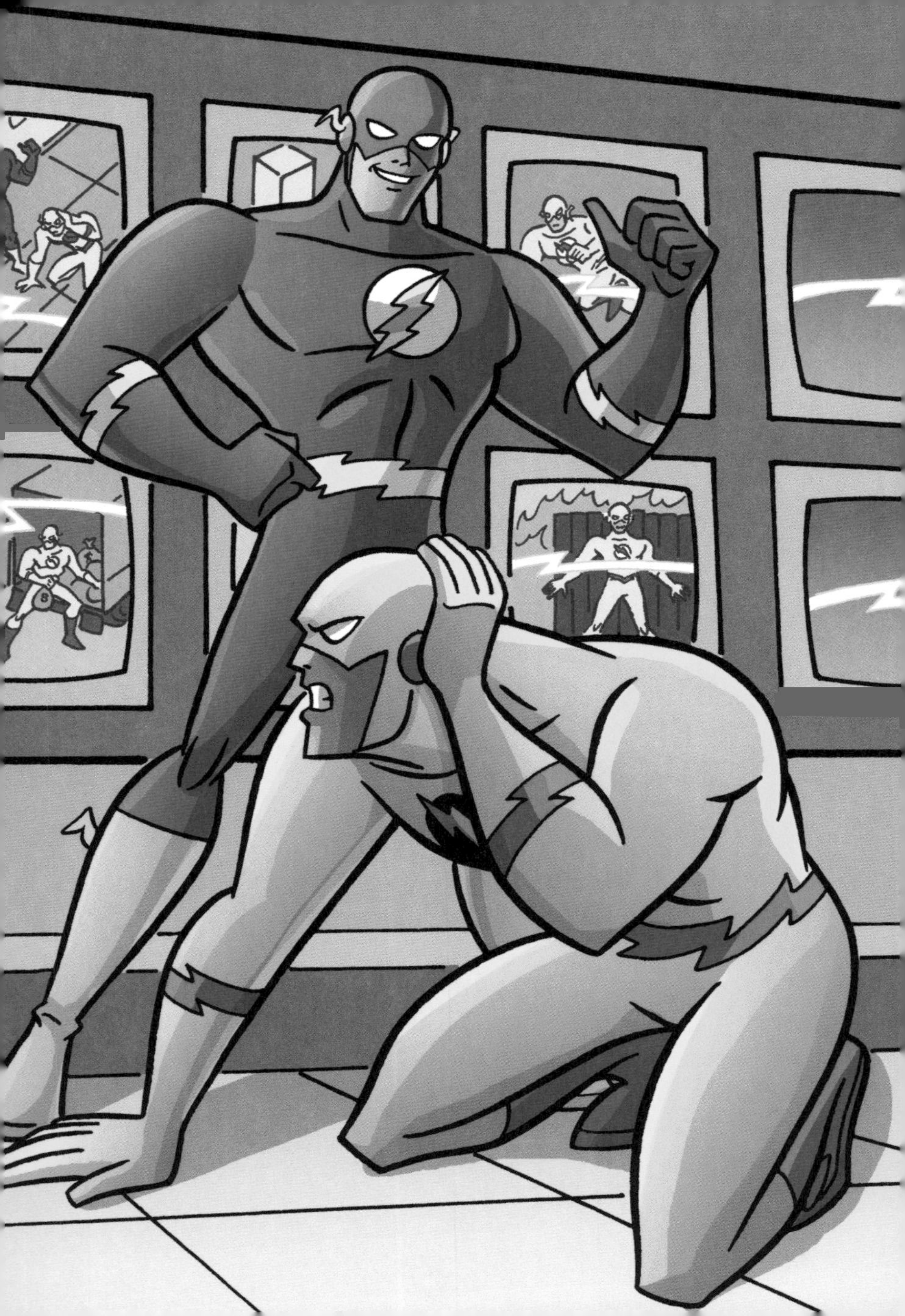

"It can handle sending a live feed to the local news stations!" Flash said. "I made sure of that before I came up here. This whole fight was caught on the security cameras. And now the public can see exactly what you were up to tonight."

Professor Zoom never got a chance to reply. The Flash wasn't about to let him. As Zoom stumbled forward, Barry punched him again, square in the jaw. **WHAM!**

Zoom fell to the ground. He was out cold and done moving.

The Flash turned around and smiled. He looked directly up at one of the museum's security cameras. "Hope you caught all that," he said. Then he picked up the Reverse-Flash and sped toward Iron Heights Penitentiary.

*   *   *

On his way home, the Flash decided
to run down Infantino Avenue again.
He paused on top of his favorite hill and
looked out over his city. The sun was just
starting to come up.

The Flash smiled. After all, Zoom was
back in his specialty cell at Iron Heights,
and the Flash's reputation was restored. All
was right with the world.

He turned and started to run again. On
his way, he passed a woman out for her
morning jog. As the red blur sped by her,
the woman smiled as her hair blew in the
wind. She knew she had just had a brush
with greatness.

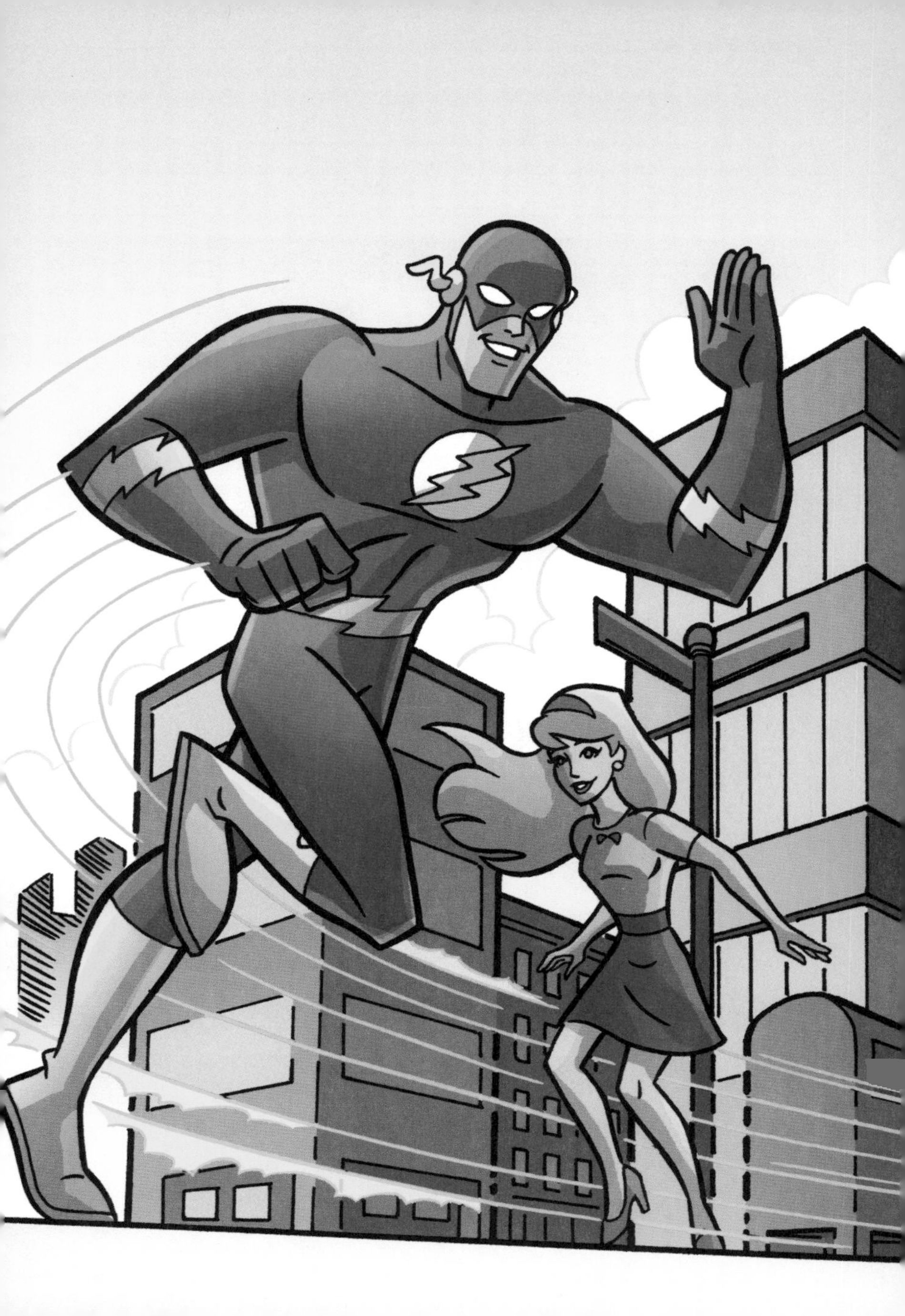

File Edit View Go Window Help

PROFESSOR ZOOM

PROFESSOR ZOOM

REAL NAME: PROFESSOR EOBARD THAWNE

OCCUPATION: PROFESSIONAL CRIMINAL

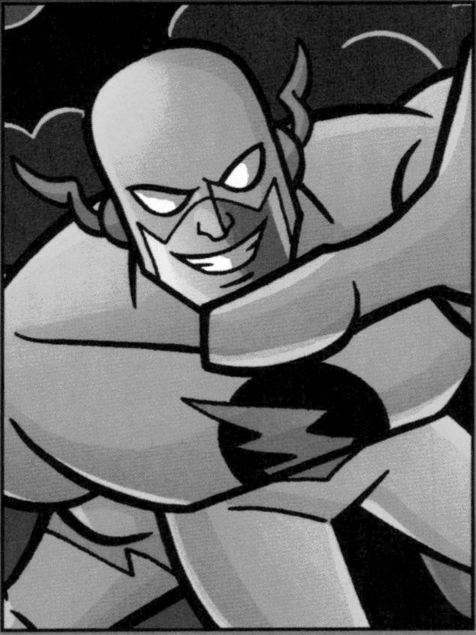

HEIGHT: 5' 11"

WEIGHT: 179 LBS.

EYES: YELLOW

HAIR: BLONDE

SPECIAL POWERS/ABILITIES:

Super-speed; a brilliant mind; made himself look just like the Flash through facial surgery.

done

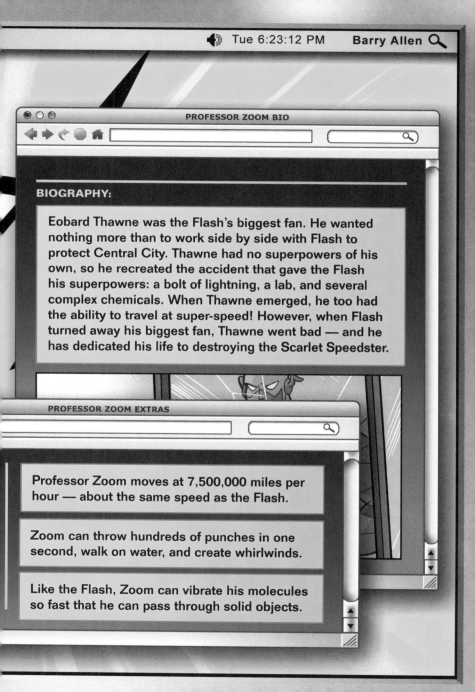

PROFESSOR ZOOM BIO

BIOGRAPHY:

Eobard Thawne was the Flash's biggest fan. He wanted nothing more than to work side by side with Flash to protect Central City. Thawne had no superpowers of his own, so he recreated the accident that gave the Flash his superpowers: a bolt of lightning, a lab, and several complex chemicals. When Thawne emerged, he too had the ability to travel at super-speed! However, when Flash turned away his biggest fan, Thawne went bad — and he has dedicated his life to destroying the Scarlet Speedster.

PROFESSOR ZOOM EXTRAS

Professor Zoom moves at 7,500,000 miles per hour — about the same speed as the Flash.

Zoom can throw hundreds of punches in one second, walk on water, and create whirlwinds.

Like the Flash, Zoom can vibrate his molecules so fast that he can pass through solid objects.

BIOGRAPHIES

Matthew K. Manning has written books or comics about Batman, Iron Man, Wolverine, the Legion of Super-Heroes, Spider-Man, the Incredible Hulk, and the Looney Tunes, including the recent hardcover history of Batman titled *The Batman Vault*. Matt lives in Brooklyn, New York, with his wife, Dorothy.

Erik Doescher is a freelance illustrator based in Dallas, Texas. He attended the School of Visual Arts in New York City. Erik illustrated for a number of comic studios throughout the 1990s, and then moved to Texas to pursue videogame development and design. However, he has not given up on illustrating his favorite comic book characters.

Mike DeCarlo is a longtime contributor of comic art whose range extends from Batman and Iron Man to Bugs Bunny and Scooby-Doo. He resides in Connecticut with his wife and four children.

Lee Loughridge has been working in comics for more than fifteen years. He currently lives in sunny California in a tent on the beach.

GLOSSARY

disturbance (diss-TURB-ance)—an interruption

evaporate (i-VAP-uh-rate)—to become less and then disappear

facility (fuh-SIL-uh-tee)—something designed or built to serve a specific function

flickered (FLIK-urd)—for a light to shine unsteadily, or go on and off

glimmering (GLIM-ur-ing)—shining faintly

havoc (HAV-uhk)—great damage and chaos

impostor (im-POSS-tur)—someone who pretends to be someone he or she is not

investigate (in-VESS-tuh-gate)—if you investigate, you find out as much as possible about something

unconscious (uhn-KON-shuhss)—not awake, or unable to see, feel, or think

vibrate (VYE-brate)—to move back and forth rapidly

DISCUSSION QUESTIONS

1. The Flash uses his super-speed to protect Central City. If you had super-speed, what would you do with it? Discuss your answers.

2. Zoom tried to trick the Flash. Have you ever fallen for a trick? Have you ever played a trick on someone? Talk about it.

3. Professor Zoom is also known as the Reverse-Flash. Do you have a nickname or other name people sometimes call you?

WRITING PROMPTS

1. Central City has an entire museum dedicated to the Flash. If you had a museum of your own, what would you put in it? Art? Sculptures? The greatest video games? Write about your museum.

2. Flash uses his superpowers for good, and Zoom uses his for evil. What does it mean to be good or evil? Can anyone be both at the same time? Write about good and evil.

3. What makes someone a hero? Is it what they do, what they say, or how they live? Can just anyone become a hero? Why or why not?

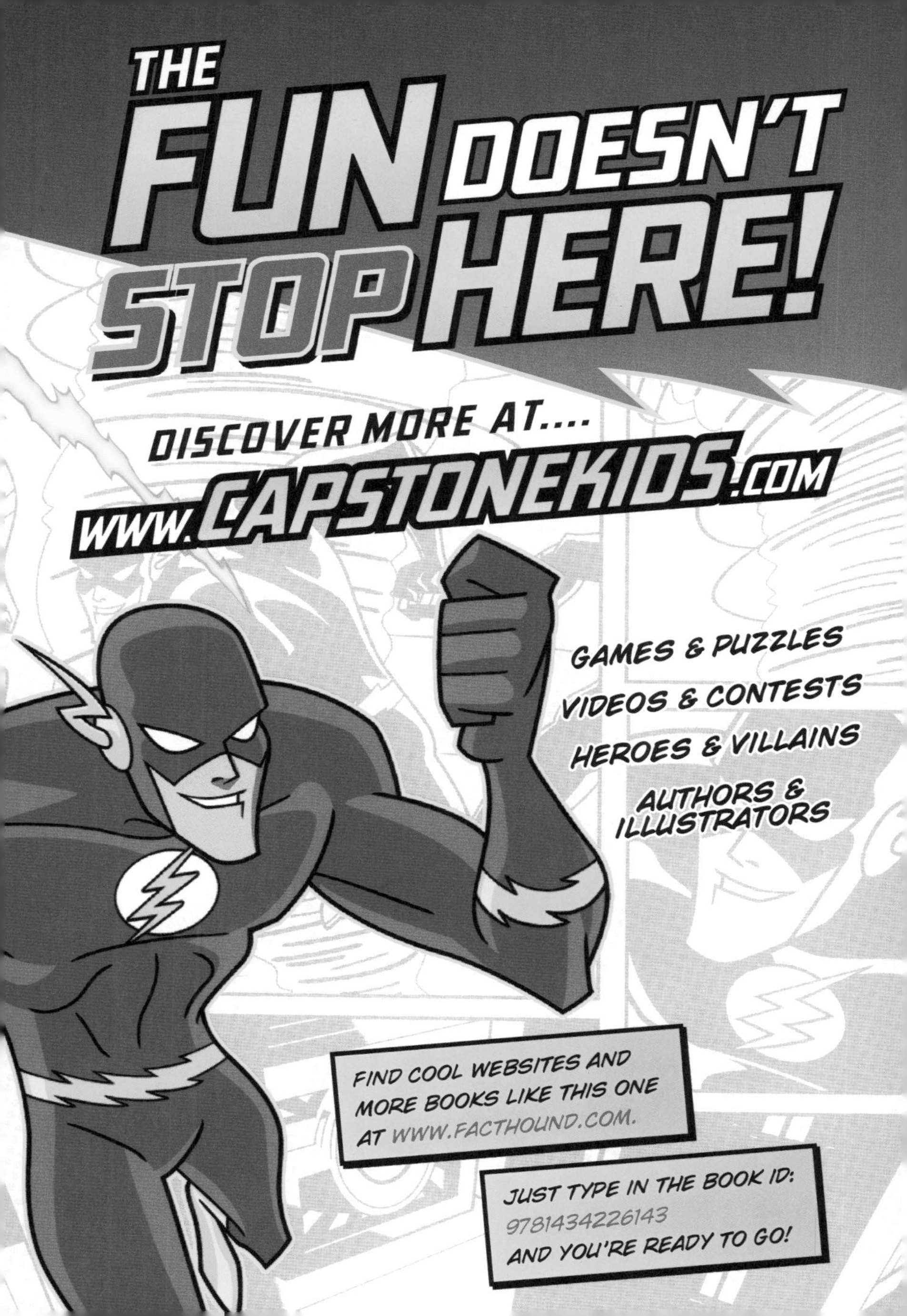
THE FUN DOESN'T STOP HERE!
DISCOVER MORE AT....
WWW.CAPSTONEKIDS.COM
GAMES & PUZZLES
VIDEOS & CONTESTS
HEROES & VILLAINS
AUTHORS & ILLUSTRATORS
FIND COOL WEBSITES AND MORE BOOKS LIKE THIS ONE AT WWW.FACTHOUND.COM.
JUST TYPE IN THE BOOK ID: 9781434226143 AND YOU'RE READY TO GO!

MORE NEW The FLASH ADVENTURES!

WRATH OF THE
WEATHER WIZARD

ATTACK OF
PROFESSOR ZOOM!

SHADOW OF THE SUN

CAPTAIN COLD'S
ARCTIC ERUPTION

GORILLA WARFARE

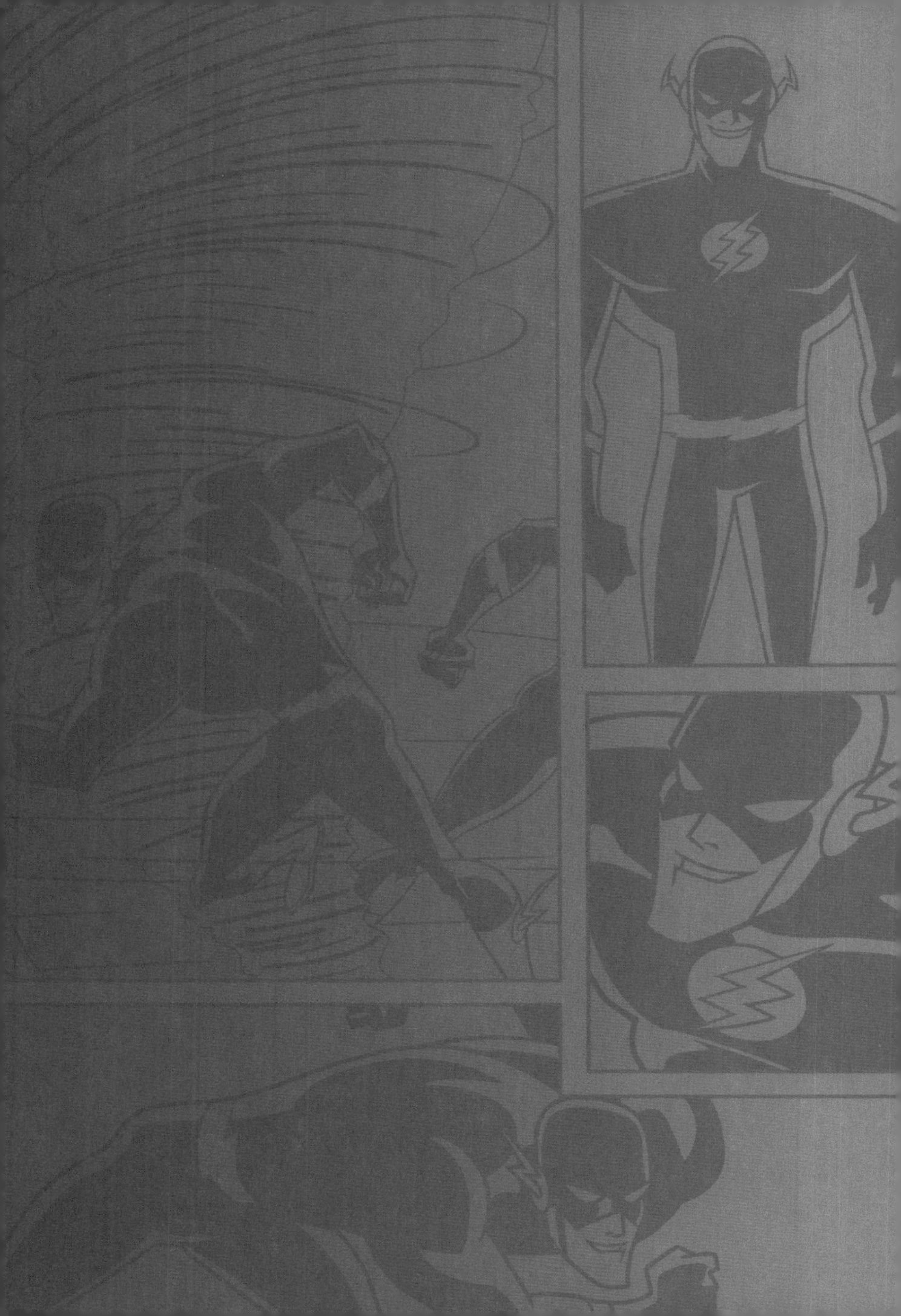

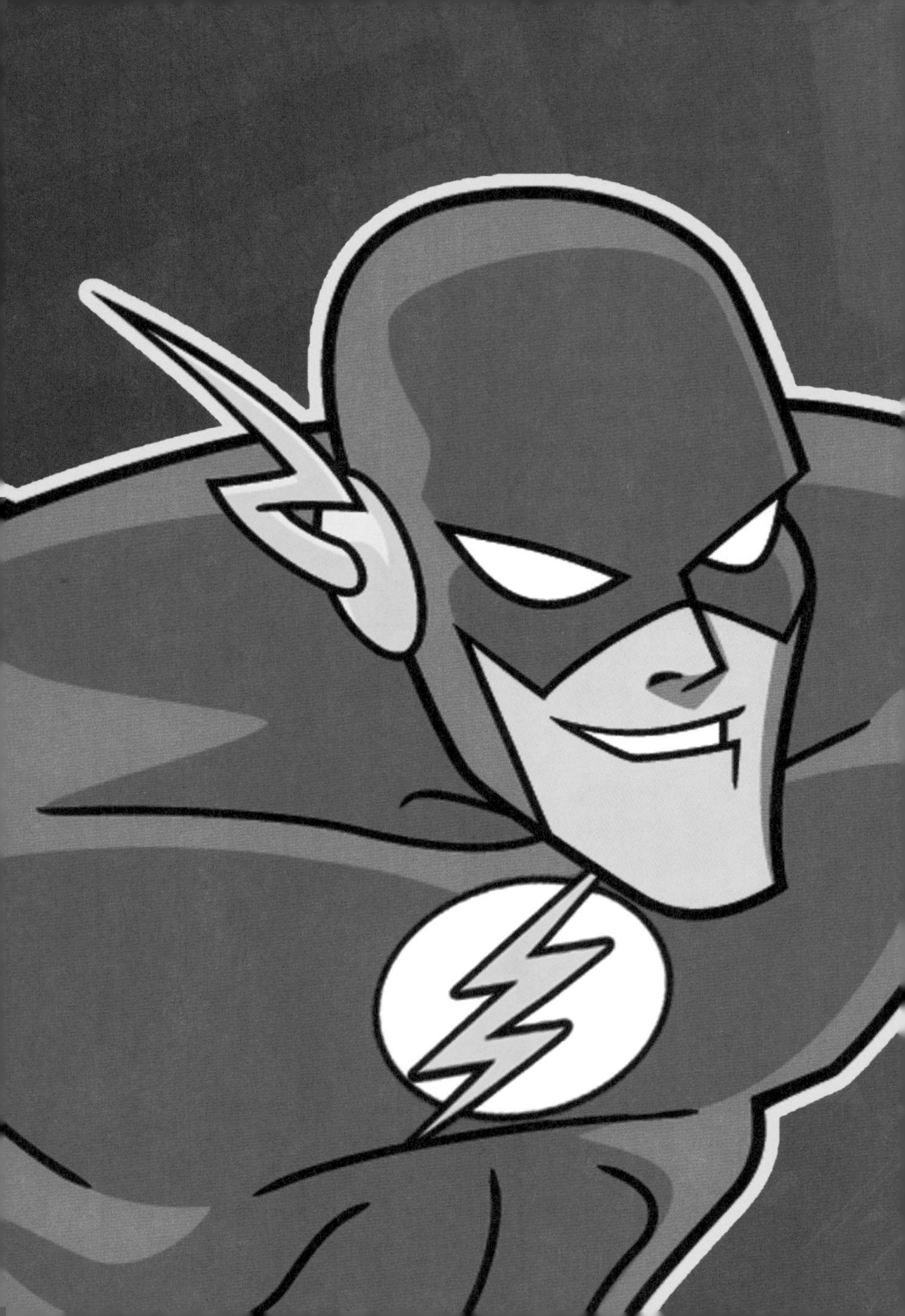

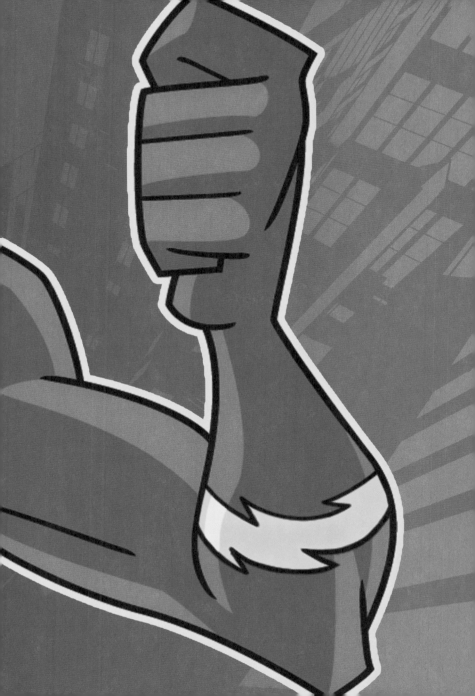